D0646499

FOOTPRINTS ON THE MOON

On July 16, 1969, the *Apollo 11* mission was launched
from Cape Canaveral, Florida. Neil Armstrong, Edwin "Buzz" Aldrin,
and Michael Collins were the astronauts chosen for the first moon landing.
On July 20, 1969, Armstrong and Aldrin stepped out of the lunar module and
walked across the dusty surface of the Sea of Tranquility. History was made.

For Gina Pollinger

M. H.

For Jake

C. B.

Author's Note

I wrote and rewrote this book a hundred times. I started out thinking it was all about orbits and escape
velocities, command modules and rock samples. I started out thinking it was all about Neil Armstrong and
Michael Collins and Buzz Aldrin. After many, many drafts that didn't work, I realized that it was a book
about all of us who sat in front of our scratchy black-and-white televisions in the summer of 1969. What
made it amazing was not the technology and the bravery and the drama. What made it amazing was the fact
that these three men had left this world and gone to another, something that had been the stuff of dreams
for thousands of years. It raises the hairs on the back of my neck, even now.

*Please note that the times referred to in this narrative are the times at which the author observed
the moon landing in the U.K.—four hours later than the times in the eastern U.S.*

Text copyright © 1996 by Mark Haddon
Illustrations copyright © 1996 by Christian Birmingham

All rights reserved. No part of this book may be reproduced, transmitted, or stored in an information retrieval system in any form or by any means,
graphic, electronic, or mechanical, including photocopying, taping, and recording, without prior written permission from the publisher.

First Candlewick Press edition 2009

First published as *The Sea of Tranquility* in Great Britain by HarperCollins Publishers Ltd. in 1996

Library of Congress Cataloging-in-Publication Data is available.

Library of Congress Catalog Card Number pending

ISBN 978-0-7636-4440-6

2 4 6 8 10 9 7 5 3 1

Printed in China

Candlewick Press
99 Dover Street
Somerville, Massachusetts 02144

visit us at www.candlewick.com

Haddon, Mark.
Footprints on the moon /

2009.
33305218779779
ca   04/14/10

FOOTPRINTS ON THE MOON

The Sea of Tranquility

Mark Haddon
illustrated by Christian Birmingham

CANDLEWICK PRESS

Years ago
there was a little boy
who had the solar system on his wall.

Late at night, he'd lie in bed
with Rabbit,
and they'd watch the planets
spinning around the sun:
Mars, the tiny space-tomato;
Saturn, sitting in its Frisbee rings;
freezing Pluto, turning slowly in the dark;
Jupiter; Uranus; Neptune; Venus; Mercury;
and Earth.

But of all the weird worlds
that whirled across his bedroom wall,
his favorite was the moon,
a small and bald and ordinary
globe of rock
that looped-the-loop
its way through outer space.

The boy leaned across his windowsill at night
and watched the moon slide up into the sky
above the smokestacks.

He borrowed his dad's binoculars
and gazed for hours
at the empty deserts
and the rocky mountains.

And it made him dizzy
just to think that he was looking
at another world
two hundred thousand miles away.

He got an atlas of the moon
for Christmas,
and he read it
like a storybook.

He dreamed of going there,
of rocketing across the cold black miles
and landing on the crumbly rock.
He dreamed of visiting
the craters in the atlas:
Prosper Henry, Klaproth, Zack.
He dreamed of driving
in a fat-tired moon-mobile
across the Bay of Rainbows
and the Sea of Rains.

He kept a scrapbook called *The Journey to the Moon*.
Inside were photographs of rockets
taking off from Cape Canaveral
and astronauts in pumped-up suits
and fishbowl helmets,
floating in zero gravity
around their little metal rooms.

He borrowed library books
and read about how astronauts
had orbited the earth
and walked in space
and how they'd flown around the moon itself.
And every night he hoped and hoped
that one day they would find a way to land
and walk across the tiny world
where he had dreamed of walking.

And eventually, one cloudless night,
they did.

He couldn't sleep.
Midnight had come and gone,
but he was wide awake
and standing at the window
in his bathrobe
because two astronauts
were walking on the surface of the moon,
two hundred thousand
miles above his bedroom.

At three a.m.
he went downstairs
and turned the television on.
And there they were
on the flickery screen,
bouncing slowly through the dust
in the Sea of Tranquility,
like giants in slow motion.

He stayed awake all night
and went to bed at dawn.
The sun was coming up
outside his window,
and the moon was fading fast.
He fell asleep,
and in his dreams
he walked with them.

That little boy was me.
I'm older now.
The solar-system wall chart
fell to pieces long ago,
and Rabbit, who is older too,
no longer follows me around
but sits beside my desk
and watches while I work.

Yet still, on cloudless nights,
I sometimes sit beside my bedroom window,
staring at that tiny, distant world.

I think how cold and dark it is up there.
No wind. No clouds. No streams. No sky.
Just rocks and dust.
I think how nothing ever moves,
year after year.

And then I think of those two astronauts,
and how the prints they made
with their big boots
will still be there
tonight,
tomorrow night,
and every night
for millions of years to come.